Silly Tilly's
VALENTINE

Silly Tilly's VALENTINE

Story and Pictures by
LILLIAN HOBAN

HarperCollins*Publishers*

HarperCollins®, 🎬®, and I Can Read Book®
are trademarks of HarperCollins Publishers Inc.

Silly Tilly's Valentine

Library of Congress Cataloging-in-Publication Data
Hoban, Lillian.
  Silly Tilly's valentine / story and pictures by Lillian Hoban.
     p.   cm. — (An I can read book)
  Summary: Mr. Bunny reminds her that the day is special, but while trying to
recall why, Silly Tilly, the forgetful mole, gets distracted by the snow.
  ISBN 0-06-027400-X. — ISBN 0-06-027401-8 (lib. bdg.)
  [1. Valentine's Day—Fiction.   2. Moles (Animals)—Fiction.   3. Snow—
Fiction.]   I. Title.   II. Series.
PZ7.H635Sin   1998   96-38239
[E]—dc20   CIP
                                                                              AC

1   2   3   4   5   6   7   8   9   10
❖
First Edition

Visit us on the World Wide Web!
http://www.harperchildrens.com

For Alisa

Silly Tilly's
VALENTINE

It was Valentine's Day.

Silly Tilly was baking cupcakes.

Brr-ring . . . Ring!

The telephone rang.

"Good morning, Tilly Mole,"

said Mr. Bunny.

"Do you remember what today is?"

"Oh, dear," said Tilly.

"I forgot to remember."

"Well, today is a special day,"
said Mr. Bunny.
"Look out the window
and you will see."
Silly Tilly looked
out the window.

"It's snowing!"

cried Tilly.

"It *is* a special day.

Just right for making a snowman!"

"Snow is nice,"

said Mr. Bunny,

"but it's not what I mean.

I will see you later."

He hung up.

"Maybe if I go outside

I will remember

why today is special,"

said Tilly.

"Then I will know
what Mr. Bunny means."
Tilly put on her boots
and her coat.

She opened the front door.

SWOOSH!

The wind swirled snow

around her.

"Goodness!" said Tilly.

"I forgot how cold snow is.

I need a scarf and mittens."

Tilly put on her scarf

and mittens.

Tilly went out in the snow.
Wherever she looked,
everything was white.
The bushes in the garden
were white.
The trees were white.
The path was white.
The mailbox at the end
of the path
was white.
But something
in the mailbox
was bright red!

"Oh," cried Tilly.

"That looks special!

Maybe that's what

Mr. Bunny means!"

Tilly ran down the path

to the mailbox.

SWISH!

She slipped.

She fell down.

"Oh, dear," said Tilly.

"I forgot to remember

how slippery snow is."

Tilly lay flat on her back.

The wind blew snow around her.

Snow fell on her face

and sprinkled her glasses.

"Goodness," said Tilly.

"It's snowing so hard,

I can't see a thing!"

Just then Mr. Mail-Mole

came to deliver some valentines.

"Tilly," he called.

"Why are you lying in the snow?
Are you making snow angels?"
Tilly blinked her eyes,
but she could not see.

"Is that you, Mr. Mail-Mole?"

she asked.

"I can't remember

why I am lying in the snow,

but I don't want

to make snow angels.

I want to make a snowman."

24

"Oh, good," said Mr. Mail-Mole.

"Wait and I will help you."

He tried to stuff the valentines

into Tilly's mailbox,

but there was no room.

Mr. Mail-Mole put Tilly's valentines

down in the snow.

"I'm ready," he said.

He started to roll a snowball.

"We will need a big snowball

for the snowman's bottom,"

he said.

"We will need a carrot

for his nose,"

said Tilly.

Tilly ran to the house

to get a carrot.

But she could not see

and the wind blew her

around and around.

She forgot where she was going.

She ran toward

the mailbox instead.

Suddenly the wind blew

Tilly's valentines up

out of the snow

and into the air.

Red hearts and pink hearts

swirled over Tilly's head.

29

"Oh!" cried Tilly.

"How lovely.

Colored snowflakes!

I will put them on the snowman

before they melt."

Tilly hurried to pick up

the snowflakes.

But she could not see

and she bumped into the mailbox.

"Is that you, Mr. Mail-Mole?"

she asked the mailbox.

"Help me put these snowflakes

on the snowman

before they melt."

"Tilly, where are you?"

called Mr. Mail-Mole.

He went up the path

to her house

and knocked on the door.

"The snowman is finished
and he needs the carrot
for his nose,"
he called.
"Oh, dear! I forgot
to remember the carrot,"
cried Tilly.

Just then Mr. Bunny

came hopping down the road.

"I will tell you

what else you forgot,"

he said.

"You forgot this."

Mr. Bunny pulled a big red heart

out of the mailbox.

"I made this valentine for you

and I wrote a poem too."

"Oh, my goodness!"

said Tilly.

"A valentine!

That's what I forgot.

I forgot to remember

it's Valentine's Day,

and I didn't make

a valentine for you."

Tilly started to sniffle.

"That's all right, Tilly,"

said Mr. Bunny.

He took out his handkerchief.

"Here, wipe your eyes."

Tilly wiped her eyes.

She wiped the snow

from her glasses.

She could see!

She read the poem

on her valentine.

It said:

Roses are red
Violets are blue
Honey is sweet
And so are you!

"That's beautiful, Mr. Bunny,"

she cried.

"Thank you!"

"These are for you too,"

said Mr. Bunny.

He picked all the red and pink

valentines up out of the snow.

"There's one from Mr. Chipmunk,
and one from Mrs. Fieldmouse,
and one from Mr. Woodchuck,
and one from . . ."

KNOCK KNOCK KNOCK!

Mr. Mail-Mole banged

on Tilly's door.

"Tilly," he called.

"Are you there?

I smell something burning!"

"Oh, my goodness!"

cried Tilly.

"I just remembered.

I didn't forget Valentine's Day.

I baked valentine cupcakes!"

43

Tilly ran to the house . . .

. . . and into the kitchen

and opened the oven door.

There were the heart-shaped cupcakes,

all golden brown and beautiful!

"It's all right," said Tilly.

"Just some crumbs burned."

Tilly iced the cupcakes

with pink icing.

Mr. Mail-Mole and Mr. Bunny

took turns licking the bowl clean.

Then they each had

a valentine cupcake.

And Mr. Mail-Mole promised
to deliver the rest
of Tilly's valentine cupcakes
to all of her friends
for Valentine's Day.